MW01140825

Mitford
at the
fashion
zoo

by Donald
Robertson

story by Kimberly Gieske

VIKING
An Imprint of Penguin Group (USA)

COVER MAGAZINE HAD a problem. Its star fashion editor, Panda Summers, needed an assistant—*fast!* Her last assistant had run away howling, and now Fashion Zoo Week was just a few days away—Panda's most busiest ever time of the whole entire year!—and her phone was *ringing ringing ringing* with fashion designers *calling calling calling*, and NO ONE to answer it.

So far, the Non-Human Resource Mouse had sent Panda exactly 521 candidates to interview. But Panda had dismissed each candidate with a *SNIFF!* "Not fabulous enough!"

"What to do? What to do?" fretted NHR Mouse.

"Isn't there *anyone* else??" asked Panda.

"Well, there is ONE LAST POSSIBILITY," said NHR Mouse. "Bring me the Mitford file!"

Mitford the Giraffe had dreamed of working for *Cover* ever since being a tiny little calf. Mitford had saved every single issue of *Cover* on a super special bedside shelf and had written letter after letter to NHR Mouse, begging for a job, *any* job, at the magazine.

Finally, NHR Mouse had agreed to see Mitford.

NON-HUMAN RESOURCES

Exactly one year ago, NHR Mouse had sent Mitford to interview with *Cover*'s creative director, Ace Salmonton. It was a DISASTER. Mitford had seen a photo by Spruce Spiderweber of a sequined feather headdress and had run up to the fancy schmancy store Bergdog Woodman and bought one to wear to the interview.

But the sequins itched. The feathers tickled. And in the middle of the interview, Mitford had a sniffly, sneezy itch attack! Needless to say, Mitford did NOT get the job. But Ace *had* admired Mitford's taste in headwear. . . .

Ring, ring! went the phone in Mitford's teensy tiny studio apartment on the Lowest East Side.

"Mitford, if you can get up to the *Cover* offices within a half hour, you've got your interview with Panda," said NHR Mouse.

Twenty minutes later, Mitford stalked into the office and stood before Panda's super chic and spotless desk. Panda looked up from the fashion layout in front of her, peered at Mitford over her Super Silly Inside Sunglasses, and declared, "Now *this* is more like it." The willowy neck, the legs for days, the cool ALOOF gaze—YES! Mitford was a fashion world NO-BRAINER.

But one of the secrets to Panda's success was that she knew that LOOKS were NOT everything.

"I have just one question for you," said Panda. "What do you think of this fashion spread?"

Mitford stared at the pictures for exactly 2.5 seconds, and then Mitford's nose began to itch. *SNIFF, SNIFF.*

"Brilliant!" declared Panda. "My thoughts exactly. You're hired." And she tossed the entire fashion shoot into the garbage.

"You're hired for a ONE-WEEK TRIAL," corrected NHR Mouse, as she showed Mitford to a desk outside Panda's office. "Tomorrow is the first day of the New York Fashion Zoo Week, where all the designers present their most fabulous new frocks. Panda will be counting on your help, so don't let her down!"

Ring, ring! went Mitford's desk phone. "This is Zap Possum," shouted a voice on the line. "I need Panda at my showroom—STAT! It's an EMERGENCY!"

Panda and Mitford RACED down to Zap's, wondering what the trouble could be. But as they approached Zap's building, the problem was plain to see: Poor Zap was standing in the street trying to squeeze one of the bags holding his OVER-THE-TOP-AMAZINGLY-CHIC dresses into the back of a cab. But the POUFFITY-POUFF skirts of Zap's big beautiful ball gowns made the bags too large to fit into even the *largest* taxi!

"Oh Panda, how will I ever get these dresses to my fashion show?" cried Zap. "Someone bring me some scissors! I'll have to cut them down to fit!"

"You'll do nothing of the sort!" said Panda. She turned to Mitford, arched her brow, and said, "Have *you* got any ideas, Mitford?"

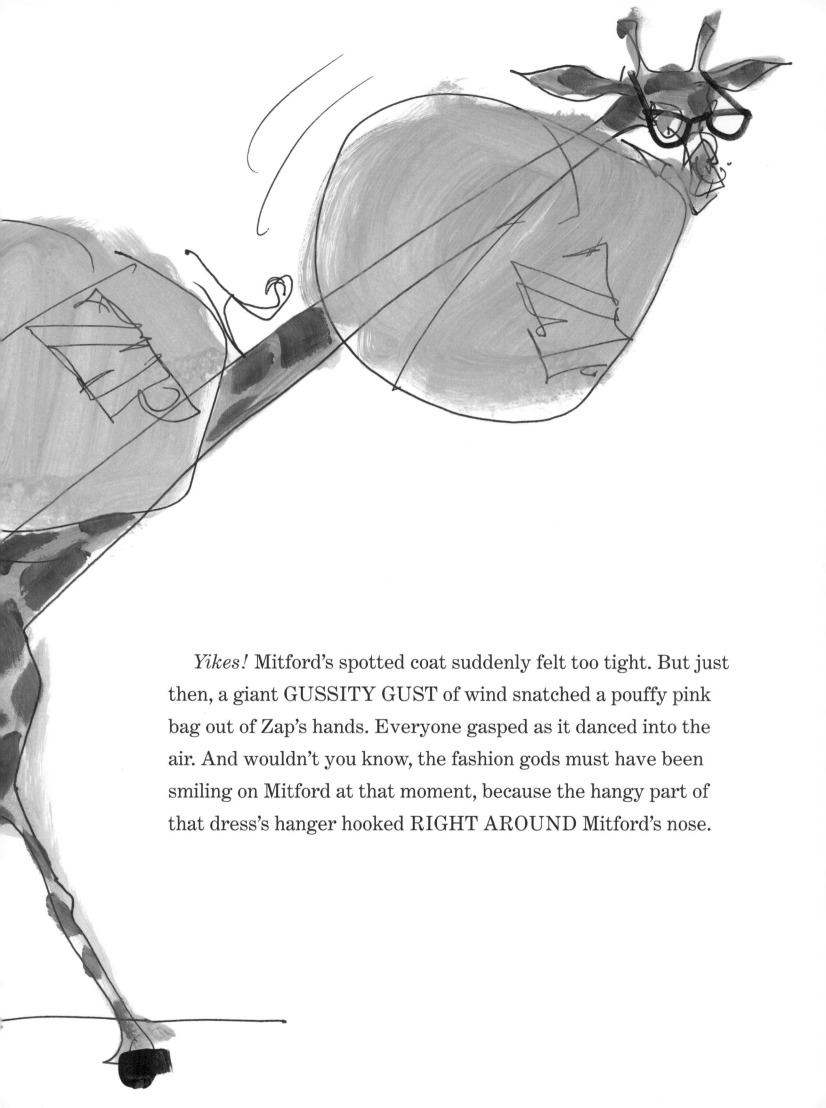

Yikes! Mitford's spotted coat suddenly felt too tight. But just then, a giant GUSSITY GUST of wind snatched a pouffy pink bag out of Zap's hands. Everyone gasped as it danced into the air. And wouldn't you know, the fashion gods must have been smiling on Mitford at that moment, because the hangy part of that dress's hanger hooked RIGHT AROUND Mitford's nose.

And then Mitford knew just what to do. The giraffe tappity-tapped a text, and moments later a group of Mitford's tallest friends appeared. Without a word, each of Mitford's friends picked up one of Zap's POUFFITY-POUFF dresses in their mouths and held them high above the trafficky street. Off they marched in a line to Zap's fashion show.

"Brilliant," proclaimed Panda.

"Kiss, kiss!" yelled Zap, before he hopped into a cab.

It was Zap's most fabulous show, maybe *ever*.

Ring, ring! went the phone on Mitford's desk the next day. "Shark Jakobs is here to see Panda!" said the voice on the line. Shark Jakobs was one of Mitford's all-time MOST FAVORITE designers. But before Mitford even had a chance to get excited, Shark flew down the hallway, past Mitford's desk, and straight into Panda's office. Mitford followed close behind.

"I have a creative BLOCK," wailed Shark to Panda. "I'm stuck! I have NO IDEAS for my show. ZILCH! NADA! NOTHING!" With that he flung himself down on Panda's pink sofa, knocking over a vase of perfectly pink peonies.

SNIFF, SNIFF, went Mitford.

SNIFF, SNIFF, went Panda.

Mitford reached for a tissue. Only it wasn't a tissue. It was a tissue-soft gazillion dollar tutu! And now it fluttered in front of Mitford like a prima ballerina.

Panda gasped.

Shark peeked through his fins. Then he sprang up in the air and straight off Panda's pink sofa—

"This is MAJOR," said Shark. "A brainy ballerina! Who wouldn't love THAT???"

"I'm seeing it," said Panda.

"Kiss, kiss!" yelled Shark as he dashed to the elevator and back downtown to his studio to design his most brilliant brainy ballerina–inspired collection, maybe *ever*.

Ring, ring! went the phone on Mitford's desk later that afternoon. "Mitford! It's time to go to the Mikael Boars show, and you're coming with me!" announced Panda. Down they went to the front of the building to hop into Panda's car.

But what's this?? NO CAR! Panda's driver was stuck in terrible traffic. Every taxi was at a stand-still. "We'll miss the show!" cried Panda.

SNIFF, SNIFF, went Mitford.

SNIFF, SNIFF, went Panda.

But Mitford knew just what to do. Mitford whipped out a Blue City Bike Card and unlocked two Blue Bikes. One for Mitford, one for Panda.

"How modern," declared Panda. (For above all, the most important thing to Panda was to be MODERN.) And off they biked to the show.

After parking their bikes, Mitford trotted along after Panda. The sidewalk was a zoo of fabulously dressed fashanimals going to the show. Mitford saw some struggling actress snake friends sipping espresso at a café. They all hissed hello.

Panda swirled to her seat at the show. But someone was already sitting in it! Mikael Boars! And he was sobbing that all the jewelry he desperately needed to go on his models had been lost by the messengers!

"Well, that's it. My show is ruined," said Mikael. And he lay down on his runway and wanted to die.

But Mitford knew just what to do. The giraffe trotted back to the struggling actress snakes, whispered in their ears, and escorted them over to the models.

"That reptile print is *everything*," announced Mikael. He threw his arms around Panda.

"It's BEYOND," declared Panda. And everyone stopped in their tracks and stared at Mitford. Because "It's BEYOND" was Panda's MOST SPECIAL COMPLIMENT, which she hardly ever ever *ever* said to *anyone!!*

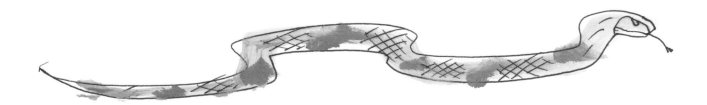

The reviews that night said that even though
the live snakes had cleared the room, it was
Mikael's most amazing show, maybe *ever*.

And with that, Mitford was BEYOND hired.
"KISS, KISS," went Panda.
"*KISS, KISS*," went Mitford.

"*KISS, KISS,*" went all of Mitford's new friends.

To Drue, Miles, Teddy, Henry, and Charlie—MY ZOO CREW —D.R.

VIKING
Published by the Penguin Group
Penguin Group (USA) LLC
375 Hudson Street
New York, New York 10014

USA • Canada • UK • Ireland • Australia
New Zealand • India • South Africa • China

penguin.com
A Penguin Random House Company

First published in the United States of America by Viking,
an imprint of Penguin Young Readers Group, 2015

Copyright © 2015 by Donald Robertson

Penguin supports copyright. Copyright fuels creativity, encourages diverse voices,
promotes free speech, and creates a vibrant culture. Thank you for buying an
authorized edition of this book and for complying with copyright laws by not reproducing,
scanning, or distributing any part of it in any form without permission. You are
supporting writers and allowing Penguin to continue to publish books for every reader.

LIBRARY OF CONGRESS CATALOGING-IN-PUBLICATION DATA IS AVAILABLE.
ISBN 978-0-451-47542-8

Manufactured in China

1   3   5   7   9   10   8   6   4   2

Set in Century Expanded

The art for this book was rendered on paper using acrylic paint, black ballpoint pen,
very magic markers, and gaffer's tape.